# Duncan Gilian

## The adventures of
## Monkey and Bean

**www.monkeyandbean.com**

**www.woodtoinspire.com**

# For my wife

Monkey and Bean in 'The Lost Dinosaur Egg' is the third in a series of illustrated children's books by Duncan Gillan following on from 'Dinosaur Footprints'. The first book in the series, 'Monkey and Bean journey to Red Island' was published in 2020.'

This story teaches the lesson to not judge others based on appearance.

Duncan Gillan is a Cabinet Maker based in London.

"My journey into writing and illustrating children's books provides an opportunity to explore a different medium of art and self-expression. It allows me to relive past adventures and throw in an imaginative twist."

Published to wide praise in 2020 Duncan's first book has proved hugely popular. "I am sincerely grateful to all who purchase my books. With the publishing of 'The Lost Dinosaur Egg', it's great to see my two favourite characters back exploring and enjoying the world."

The book features 22 full page, colour hand drawn and painted illustrations. Included are three fun educational questions to support learning at the end of the story.

www.monkeyandbean.com

www.woodtoinspire.com

"We better hurry Bean or we will miss the train. The train leaves only once a week so if we miss this one, we will have to stay here."

Monkey and Bean ran for the train.

The train blew its whistle encouraging our two heroes to board as quickly as possible.

With just minutes to spare, Monkey and Bean got on the train.

The train was bright red with very long blue carriages which stretched into the distance, further than Monkey and Bean could see.

Bean wondered how long it would take to build such a big train, while Monkey just wanted to sit and eat bananas.

"Let us sit here," said Monkey.

Monkey and Bean sat on the train and ate a breakfast of bananas and nuts, sharing a giant banana milkshake.

"Let us sit at this table shall we Bean, said Monkey."

Monkey and Bean eat their breakfast whilst looking out of the window. As the train began to move it signalled the start of another exciting adventure for our two friends.

"I cannot wait to see Dinosaur, can you Monkey? Though Dinosaur does look sad when we look in the Ruby."

Monkey and Bean stared into the ruby, that Dinosaur had given them as a gift the last time that they were in the mountains.

Dinosaur was sitting still, looking gloomy, tearful and lost.

The train continued to snake its way through the mountains passing many trees and over wild un-tamed rivers. Monkey wondered where all the banana trees were.

Fresh air blew through the windows of the train. It brought with it the smell of the trees and mountains that soaked up the sun's rays in the beautiful land of dinosaurs.

The train snaked its way through the mountains, through tunnels passing many trees and over wild un-tamed rivers. Monkey wondered where all the banana trees were.

Fresh air blew through the train windows. Monkey and Bean smelled the welcome scent of pine trees and enjoyed the mountain views in the beautiful land of dinosaurs.

After spending two days and nights on the train, Monkey and Bean arrived at their destination.

They walked into the mountains on their way to find their good Friend, Dinosaur. After a while they came across the perfect location to rest and build a fire.

"This looks like the perfect place for us to pitch our tent and build a fire, before it gets dark, Bean. Then tomorrow we will search for Dinosaur."

Monkey and Bean pitched their tent by the edge of a river with a waterfall in the background. The noise was very relaxing, and later helped our friends sleep.

"Let us rest, Monkey and then we will go in search of Dinosaur."

Monkey and Bean toasted their bananas over the fire, before going to sleep in their tent.

"Careful Monkey, or you will burn your banana...."

"Ooh, hot. Yum, yum"

Page 11

Monkey and Bean awoke the next day well rested and keen to see Dinosaur.

"If we use this canoe, Monkey, we will get to Dinosaur quicker."

"I can paddle but you will need to map read, please Bean."

Monkey was exceptionally good at canoeing. Monkey pedalled so fast that the front of the canoe rose out of the water giving Bean a clear view of where they were going.

Giant fishes could be seen swimming in the direction they were heading. It was almost as if the fishes were showing Monkey and Bean the way.

"I see Dinosaur," commented Bean as they approached the island.

Our adventurers arrived at the place where Dinosaur lived. It was a small island in the middle of a great big lake surrounded by trees and mountains. The sun shone brightly illuminating the water a bright blue colour.

"Wow you are both here. I knew you would come. It is great to see you both."

"It is very good to be here," replied Bean and Monkey.

"If you don't mind us saying, you look a little sad. Have you run out of bananas? We have plenty to share if you would like one and Bean has some peanuts".

Our adventurers arrived at the place where Dinosaur lived.

"Hey Dinosaur, so good to see you again."

"Dinosaur, why do you look so sad? We have bananas…."

"Thank you, my friends. I have plenty to eat. I am sad because my egg has disappeared. There are not many of my kind left in the world and this egg was our future"

"Where do you think it has gone? asked Bean"

"I think Turd Bird has flown off with it. Will you both help me look for it?"

"Of course, we will help you, Dinosaur. And Bean has a magnifying glass that might help find clues."

Every so often, the three friends came across a huge mound of steaming poo.

"Interesting", said Bean. You see these large mounds of poo. A very large bird might have dropped them. I think we need to follow the poo, don't you.

"Onwards, friends, we must follow the poo trail." Monkey said enthusiastically.

"The poo mounds are getting bigger," said Dinosaur.

"We must be getting closer to the poo makers location. I think the mounds must have been made by 'Turd Bird."

"Monkey, Dinosaur. Look, there on top of that large rock…."

"It is my egg," said Dinosaur excitedly.

Monkey and Dinosaur looked up in the direction Bean was pointing at.

"That is, it. There is the egg" said Dinosaur, who was clearly very excited and relieved. "But how will we get it when it is on the top of that rock?"

"I have an idea," suggested Bean. If Dinosaur pulls down that treetop, which Monkey can hold on to, we can catapult him to the top of the rock. What do you think?"

"Great idea, Bean," replied Monkey and Dinosaur.

Dinosaur Grabbed onto the end of the tree and pulled it into position while Monkey climbed on.

"One, two, three, let gooooooooooooo." Monkey's words were stretched out as he was catapulted high into the sky, taking a rucksack to carry the egg in when he climbed back down.

What none of them saw though, was a huge bird with a giant beak approaching……!

"Wow, I am flying",
thought Monkey.
"Could I be the first
Ape in Space?"

"Wow, I am flying", thought Monkey. "Could I be the first Ape in Space?"

Monkey landed on the hoodoo and shouted down to Bean and Dinosaur.

"I have the egg. I will climb down now."

Monkey grabbed the huge egg, which had a crack in it and scooped it into the rucksack. It was a very tight fit and Monkey had to eat some bananas just to make room for it.

*Page 26*

When Monkey got to the ground, he was reunited with his friends who could hear a loud farting noise.

"Was you scared up there, Monkey?" asked Dinosaur.

"What is that smell?" asked Bean.

"It must be Turd Bird," said Monkey.

"Quickly run and hide…." suggested Dinosaur "before Turd Bird finds us."

But it was too late, and Turd Bird started to follow them.

Our three friends began to run away in the direction that they had come from, but Turd Bird followed and when flapping its wings, farted very loudly.

"Run my friends, run. Turd Bird is coming," shouted Dinosaur.

"Bean, Dinosaur; sit on this log and we can ride it to the bottom of the mountain."

The three friends reached the top of a mountain covered in snow.

"Bean, Dinosaur; sit on this log and we can ride it to the bottom of the mountain."

As they slid down the slope, they got quicker and quicker, but could not escape Turd Bird who continued to follow them.

Monkey, Bean and Dinosaur reached the bottom and continued to run away from Dinosaur.

They reached the edge of a large cliff overlooking a lake, Monkey, Bean and Dinosaur had no-where to go. They could not run any further without a long difficult climb. Monkey would have to carry all of them down the cliff face, one at a time.


"STOP BEAN, STOP DINOSAUR……..", shouted Monkey.


Turd Bird had them cornered. There was nothing that they could do. Would they have to give Turd Bird back the egg?

The three friends came to a cliff
and could not run any further.

"STOP BEAN, STOP DINOSAUR"

"Hi, please don't run. I don't mean to smell. I found the egg and did not know what to do with it, so I thought I would look after it and help it to hatch. Could we all be pals?"

"Sorry we ran away," replied Dinosaur.

"We would love to be your friend," said Monkey.

Monkey and Bean, Dinosaur and his egg and Turd Bird walked back to Dinosaur's home.

When they got to Dinosaur's home the egg started to hatch.

It was a perfect day and the sun begin to shine on the dinosaur as the baby dinosaur hatched into world. The sun was especially bright warming the friends as they looked on excitedly.

"After all that excitement I feel very hungry, said Monkey. "Let's all have a Banana and celebrate. Then I will teach you how to do the monkey dance"

The friends all eat their banana's and welcomed Baby Dinosaur into the world.

Legend has it that when good friends walk underneath an archway of trees together, they can be transported anywhere their minds can imagine.

It was time for Monkey and Bean to leave, and as they passed under the trees not knowing where they were going, waving goodbye to their friends, they knew they would not forget the dinosaurs and Turd Bird.

They knew that they would see them again and could visit whenever they liked so long as they continue to believe and look into the magic Ruby, Dinosaur had once given them.

# The End

*Monkey and Bean will return in,*
*'The Dog Catcher of Dubrovnik'*

# Counting and spelling fun

- How many bananas are growing on this tree?

- Write the missing letters in these words?

## _o_k_y and B__n

- How many bananas does Monkey have?

🍌🍌 **X** 🍌🍌🍌 **=**

# Locations featured in 'The Lost Dinosaur Egg'

Monkey and Bean in 'The Lost Dinosaur Egg' is the third in a series of illustrated children's books by Duncan Gillan following on from 'Dinosaur Footprints'. The first book in the series, 'Monkey and Bean journey to Red Island' was published in 2020.

Duncan Gillan is a Cabinet Maker based in London.

"My journey into writing and illustrating children's books provides an opportunity to explore a different medium of art and self-expression. It allows me to relive past adventures and throw in an imaginative twist."

Published to wide praise in 2020 Duncan's first book has proved hugely popular. "I am sincerely grateful to all who purchase my books. With the publishing of 'The Lost Dinosaur Egg', it's great to see my two favourite characters back exploring and enjoying the world."

The book features 22 full page, colour hand drawn and painted illustrations. Included are three fun educational questions to support learning at the end of the story.

www.monkeyandbean.com

www.woodtoinspire.com

Printed by Amazon Italia Logistica S.r.l.
Torrazza Piemonte (TO), Italy

Printed by Amazon Italia Logistica S.r.l.
Torrazza Piemonte (TO), Italy

47712038R00025